BLAZERS

SUPER SPEED

MOTORCYCLE Racing

BY LORI POLYDOROS

Reading Consultant:
Barbara J. Fox
Reading Specialist
Professor Emerita
North Carolina State University

CAPSTONE PRESS
a capstone imprint

Blazers Books are published by Capstone Press,
1710 Roe Crest Drive, North Mankato, Minnesota 56003
www.capstonepub.com

Library of Congress Cataloging-in-Publication Data

Polydoros, Lori, 1968–

Motorcycle racing / by Lori Polydoros.

pages cm.—(Blazers. Super speed.)

Includes bibliographical references and index.

Summary: "Describes safety features and rules governing different types of motorcycle races, including Moto Grand Prix races, supermoto races, and enduro races"—Provided by publisher.

ISBN 978-1-4765-0121-5 (library binding)

ISBN 978-1-4765-3369-8 (ebook PDF)

1. Motorcycle racing—Juvenile literature. I. Title.

GV1060.P638 2014

796.7'5—dc23 2013003671

Editorial Credits

Gene Bentdahl, designer; Jennifer Walker, production specialist

Photo Credits

Alamy: Goddard Automotive, 27; Corbis: Steve Bardens, 7; Newscom: Cal Sport Media/Danny Reise, 10-11, Cal Sport Media/William Mancebo, cover, EPA/Maxim Shipenkov, 13, Icon SMI CBB/Dannie Walls, 25, MCT/Contra Costa Times/Jose Carlos Fajardo, 5, PhotoPQR/Nice Matin, 18, 19, ZUMA Press/Clay Morrison, 26, ZUMA Press/SCG/Matt Gdowski, 23; Shutterstock: B.Stefanov, 16, Diego Barbieri, 8-9, 29, haak78, 20–21, Rainer Herhaus, 14, Sportsphotographer.eu, 17

Artistic Effects

Shutterstock: 1xpert, My Portfolio, rodho

Capstone Press thanks Peter terHorst for sharing his motorcycling expertise during the production of this book.

Printed in the United States of America in Stevens Point, Wisconsin.
032013 007227WZF13

TABLE OF CONTENTS

FULL SPEED AHEAD

Motorcycle racing is all about action and speed. **Off-road** motorcycle racers ride on dirt tracks, through woods, and across deserts. Road racers compete on long, **paved** courses. Motorcycles are built differently for off-road and paved courses.

off-road—describes a vehicle built to operate away from public streets and roads

paved—when a surface is covered with a hard material such as concrete or asphalt

FAST FACT

The American Motorcyclist Association (AMA) is the world's largest motorcycling organization.

BUILT TO RACE

Motocross racers push dirt bikes to their limits. These bikes have powerful engines and strong **suspensions**. Riders use skill and strength to climb hills, charge into corners, and sail over jumps.

motocross—a sport in which people race motorcycles on outdoor dirt tracks

suspension—the system that helps smooth out the up and down movements as a vehicle goes over bumps

FAST FACT

The main professional motocross series in the United States is the AMA Pro Motocross Championship.

In Supercross races, riders race dirt bikes on tracks in indoor stadiums. Riders soar over jumps and speed over **whoops**.

whoops—a series of bumps on a motocross or Supercross track

FAST FACT

AMA Supercross is the most watched type of motorcycle racing in the United States.

Flat track racers zip around flat oval tracks. Their bikes have powerful engines but no front **brakes**. Riders slide through turns and use their foot to balance.

brake—equipment that slows down or stops a vehicle

FAST FACT

Flat track riders race at speeds of nearly 140 miles (225 kilometers) per hour.

Road racing motorcycles are tuned-up **production** motorcycles or racing **prototypes**. Full **fairings** help the bikes cut through the air. Riders compete on twisty paved tracks.

production—describes a vehicle made to be sold to the public

prototype—an early model of a vehicle made to test and improve the design; motorcycle prototypes race in the Moto Grand Prix (MotoGP) World Championship series

fairing—a shell placed over the frame of a motorcycle to reduce air drag

FAST FACT

The Daytona 200 is the most famous road race in the United States. The motorcycles can reach 200 miles (322 km) per hour.

Prototype motorcycles face off in Moto Grand Prix (MotoGP) road races. MotoGP is split into classes based on engine size. Top riders from around the world compete in this popular series.

FAST FACT

More than 2 million people attended MotoGP races in 2012.

Supermoto races take place on tracks with both paved and dirt sections. The motorcycles are similar to dirt bikes, but they have road-racing tires.

FAST FACT

Supermoto tracks have the jumps of motocross tracks and the sliding corners of dirt tracks.

FAST FACT

World Championship enduro courses are at least 124 miles (200 km) long.

Enduro racers have been competing since 1913. Riders in enduro races try to reach the end of a course in a set amount of time.

1
2
3
4
YAMAHA
BRIDGESTONE

PHOTO DIAGRAM

1. POWERFUL ENGINE
2. EXHAUST PIPE
3. SMOOTH TIRES
4. FAIRINGS
5. STRONG DISC BRAKES
6. TOUGH SUSPENSION
7. WINDSHIELD

THE QUICKEST CYCLES

Motorcycle drag racers zoom down a paved drag strip 0.25 mile (0.4 km) long. Racers compete in classes based on engine size in the National Hot Rod Association (NHRA) Championship Motorcycle Series.

FAST FACT

For the NHRA Pro Stock Motorcycle category, bikes are specially built. They look very different from street versions.

Drag racing bikes are built low to the ground for **stability**. They have the most powerful engines of all racing motorcycles. Large rear tires give them added **traction**.

stability—likely to stay upright

traction—the gripping power that holds a vehicle's tires to the ground

IMPACT!
FRAM
PROGRESSIVE

Land speed racing is all about flat land and top speeds. Racers ride specially built motorcycles. Land speed bikes can reach speeds of 300 miles (483 km) per hour or more.

1350 CC 6061
XLFORUM.NET
landracing.com

A WINNING COMBINATION

Motorcycle racers need strength, skill, and courage as they battle for the win. The many thrills of motorcycle racing make it one of the most popular motorsports today.

151

GLOSSARY

brake (BRAYK)—equipment that slows down or stops a vehicle

fairing (FAYR-ing)—a shell placed over the frame of a motorcycle to reduce air drag

motocross (MOH-toh-kross)—a sport in which people race motorcycles on outdoor dirt tracks

off-road (OFF-ROHD)—describes a vehicle built to operate away from public streets and roads

paved (PAYVED)—when a surface is covered with a hard material such as concrete or asphalt

production (pruh-DUHK-shuhn)—describes a vehicle made to be sold to the public

prototype (PROH-tuh-tipe)—an early model of a vehicle made to test and improve the design; motorcycle prototypes race in the MotoGP World Championship series

stability (stuh-BI-luh-tee)—likely to stay upright

suspension (suh-SPEN-shuhn)—the system that helps smooth out the up and down movements as a vehicle goes over bumps

traction (TRAK-shuhn)—the gripping power that holds a vehicle's tires to the ground

whoops (WOOPS)—a series of bumps on a motocross or Supercross track

READ MORE

Adamson, Thomas K. *Motocross Racing.* Dirt Bike World. Mankato, Minn.: Capstone Press, 2011.

Georgiou, Tyrone. *Pro Stock Motorcycle Dragsters.* New York: Gareth Stevens, 2011.

Ruck, Colleen. *Motorcycles.* My Favorite Machines. Mankato, Minn.: Smart Apple Media, 2011.

Tieck, Sarah. *Superbikes.* Edina, Minn.: ABDO Publishing, 2011.

Von Finn, Denny. *Drag Racing Motorcycles.* Minneapolis: Bellwether Media, 2011.

INTERNET SITES

FactHound offers a safe, fun way to find Internet sites related to this book. All of the sites on FactHound have been researched by our staff.

Here's all you do:

Visit *www.facthound.com*

Type in this code: 9781476501215

INDEX